MADDIE AND MABEL

For Kelsey, the Mabel to my Maddie always. –K.A.

To Nora and Louisa, my favorite pair of sisters. –T.M.

Maddie and Mabel is published by
Kind World Publishing, PO Box 22356, Eagan, MN 55122
www.kindworldpublishing.com

Text copyright © 2022 by Kari Allen
Illustrations copyright © 2022 by Tatjana Mai-Wyss
Cover illustrations copyright © 2022 by Tatjana Mai-Wyss
Cover design by Tim Palin Creative
Book design by Katherine Liestman

Published in 2022 by Kind World Publishing.

Printed in China.
Second printing, 2022.

ISBN 978-1-63894-002-9 (hardcover)
ISBN 978-1-63894-009-8 (ebook)

Library of Congress Cataloging-in-Publication Data is available
on the Library of Congress website.
Library of Congress Control Number: 2021923348

Maddie and Mabel

By Kari Allen

Illustrated by Tatjana Mai-Wyss

Kind World
PUBLISHING
Eagan, Minnesota

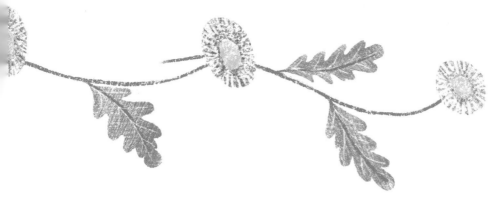

CHAPTERS

SISTERS

Maddie and Mabel are sisters.

Maddie is the big sister.

Mabel is the little sister.

Maddie tries to do things herself.

Mabel tries to help.

Maddie likes to be in charge.

Mabel likes to ask questions.

Mabel and Maddie are sisters.

THE RABBIT

"Maddie, will you tell me again about the rabbit?" Mabel asked her big sister.

"Before it was you and me, it was just me," said Maddie.

"Before it was me and you, it was just you?" asked Mabel.

"Yes," said Maddie.

"Were you lonely?" asked Mabel.

"Sometimes," said Maddie.

"What happened next?" asked Mabel.

"Our parents asked me a question,"
said Maddie.

"An important question?" asked Mabel.

"*Very* important," said Maddie.
"They asked: would you rather have
a baby sister or a pet rabbit?"

"I like rabbits," said Mabel.

"Me too," said Maddie.

"Now tell which one you picked,"
said Mabel.

"I picked the rabbit," said Maddie.

"Why?" asked Mabel.

"Rabbits are cute and small. Rabbits wiggle their noses," said Maddie.

"I'm cute! I'm small! I wiggle my nose!" shouted Mabel.

"They are also quiet," said Maddie and she looked at Mabel.

"I'm quiet," whispered Mabel.

"We don't have a rabbit," said Mabel.

"No, we don't. I got you instead,"
said Maddie. "I'm glad."

"Me too," said Mabel.

And she hopped
around the room.

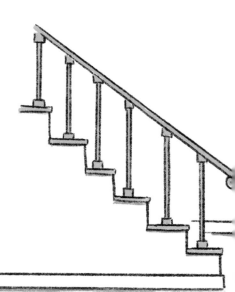

THE SHOW

One day Maddie and Mabel decided to put on a show.

"What do we need to do to have a show?" asked Mabel.

"We will need costumes," said Maddie. "I will make them."

"What else do we need?" asked Mabel.

"We will need songs," said Maddie.

"All good shows have songs," said Mabel.

"Yes," said Maddie. "I will write them."

Mabel thought.

"We will need a stage!" said Mabel.

"Yes," said Maddie. "I will build it."

"What can I do?" asked Mabel.

Maddie shrugged.

Maddie made costumes.

Mabel thought.

Maddie wrote songs.

Mabel thought.

Maddie built a stage.

Mabel thought.

"We are ready!" said Maddie. "We are ready
for our show!"

"I think we are forgetting something,"
said Mabel.

"We have the best costumes! We have great
songs! We have a strong stage. We have
everything we need," said Maddie.

Mabel shrugged.

Maddie started the show.

She stood on her stage.

She wore her costumes.

She sang her songs.

When Maddie was done, she took a big bow.

But no one clapped.

Maddie looked up.

"I knew we forgot something.
Something important," said Mabel.

"We forgot the audience," said Maddie.

"We weren't ready after all," said Mabel.

"No," said Maddie.

"No one's ready the first time," said Mabel.

"No," said Maddie. "Probably not."

"Next time I want to be in the show,"
said Mabel.

"Next time we'll be ready," said Maddie.

Maddie took another bow and this time
Mabel clapped.

THE FIGHT

Mabel was mad.

Mabel was really mad at Maddie.

Maddie was always in charge.

Maddie always got to pick everything.

"Do you want to do another show?"
asked Maddie.

"No," said Mabel.

"Do you want to play a game?"
asked Maddie.

"No," said Mabel.

"What do you want to do?" asked Maddie.

"Nothing," said Mabel. "I am mad."

"When I am mad, playing always helps,"
said Maddie.

Mabel did not want to play.

"When I'm mad, thinking of something silly
always helps," said Maddie.

Mabel did not want to be silly.

"I don't want to play. I don't want to laugh.
I want to be alone," said Mabel and she left.

Maddie went to play by herself.

She tried playing catch.

She tried playing cards.

She even tried playing rabbits.

It was not the same.

Maddie tried to be silly.

She stuck out her tongue.

She wiggled her arms and legs.

She made every funny face
she could think of.

It was really not the same.

Maddie went to find Mabel.

Maddie knocked on Mabel's door.

Maddie waited.

No sounds came from behind the door.

Maddie tried again.

"Mabel?" asked Maddie.

Maddie waited.

Mabel did not answer.

Maddie tried another way.

Maddie slid a note for Mabel under the door.

I'm sorry.

Maddie waited until Mabel opened the door.

"You are still not the boss," said Mabel.

"I know," said Maddie.

"Want to play?" asked Mabel.

"Always," said Maddie.

AWAKE

Maddie was asleep.

Mabel was not.

She was awake, really awake.

"Maddie?" whispered Mabel.

Maddie did not move.

Maddie did not even wiggle.

Mabel tried again.

"Maddie," Mabel said.

Mabel poked Maddie.

"Maddie are you asleep?"

"Yes," Maddie said.

"I can't sleep," Mabel said.

"Why not?" asked Maddie.

"I am thinking," said Mabel.

"Stop thinking. Go to sleep," said Maddie.

"I can't stop thinking," said Mabel. "I have too many ideas."

"Try counting something," said Maddie.

"Like rabbits?" asked Mabel.

"Maybe try to count your ideas,"
said Maddie.

"Maddie!" said Mabel.

"Yes?" asked Maddie.

"Counting my ideas isn't working,"
said Mabel. "I still can't sleep."

"How many ideas do you have?"
asked Maddie.

"What comes after forty-two?" asked Mabel.

"Forty-three," said Maddie.

"Forty-three," said Mabel. "I have
forty-three ideas."

"Wow. That is a lot of ideas," said Maddie.

"I still can't sleep," said Mabel.

"Do you want to hear a story?"
asked Maddie.

"Yes," said Mabel.

"What kind of story?" asked Maddie.

"A good one," said Mabel.

"I'll tell you the best story," said Maddie.
"I'll tell you our story."

Mabel wiggled in next to Maddie.

"Before it was you and me, it was just me.
Then one day our parents asked me
a question. A very important question,"
said Maddie.

And as Maddie told their story,
Mabel finally fell asleep.

TALK ABOUT IT

Maddie and Mabel is about two sisters and the things they do together. What are some of the things you like to do with people you care about? Why do you enjoy those activities?

Maddie and Mabel often talk about "their story" and the rabbit. What family stories do you have that you tell often? How does it make you feel when you hear those stories or share them with others?

MAKE A KINDER WORLD

In this story, Maddie has to apologize to Mabel. How do you feel when you have to apologize to someone? What makes a good apology? How do you feel when someone apologizes to you?

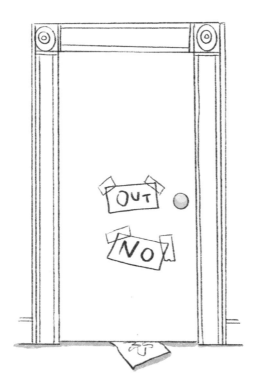

CONNECT TO YOUR STORY

Maddie and Mabel make up a play together. If you were to make up a play like the girls do in this story, what would yours be about? Try writing or drawing some of it!